# LIFE IS DEATH

AARYA SARAF

ISBN 979-888569169-7

# Contents

# Contents

# Foreword

I had the unique pleasure of reading Aarya Saraf's first book, 'Criminal Minds', a couple of years back and was intrigued with the thriller genre he had so diligently pursued and the gripping plot that he had creatively imagined. I am honoured yet again, to have the incredible distinction of going through his second book, ' Life is Death' and am impressed with the transforming journey Aarya has made from a young student at Suncity School, testing new waters as a writer, to an evolving young adult writer.

The first page itself has you hooked on to the roller coaster ride one is about to embark on. The turning of pages entangles the immersed reader in a high octave emotion and action web so much that one becomes a part of the story, such is the realism in the captivating narration.

Way to go, Aarya! Another feather in your over adorned cap of achievements! I am sure we will be eagerly awaiting for sequels of your publications in the near future. Rise and shine, Sweets!

Sapna Bakshi

Educator, Suncity School

# Acknowledgements

Firstly, I would like to thank my parents for always being my side and continously supporting me in such endeavours.

I'm grateful to my teachers and my school, Suncity School who helped me become who I am today and built my foundations from the ground up. Especially Ms. Sapna Bakshi ma'am, for always being enthusiastic about everything I do, proofreading my manuscript and writing the foreword. None of this would've been possible without you.

I would also like to thank my friends who have helped me in this journey and reviewing my book.

Especially Lakshya, who constantly tolerated me asking him for reviews after every chapter I wrote and editing them for me.

Lastly, thanks to Notionpress for bringing my book to life.

# Caution!

Hello, Anonymous Reader! Whether you're just a fellow human having half an existential crisis or a curious guy who found this book lost somewhere in the ruins of time, trust me, you don't want to read this! This book has secrets, dark secrets, truths unknown and memories swept away. I don't know why I'm writing this, or for who but this is my journal. Or if I ever get famous, you could probably get it published as a book too. Eh, not sure how good an idea that is, considering the contents of this book but if you still wish to continue reading, beware!

..........and well, I hope you come out of this alive.

LAST WARNING: You either leave now or go through this alone, the choice is yours!

It seems like you have what most don't.

Courage!

And now that you've embarked on this journey, I wish you a safe flight anyway!

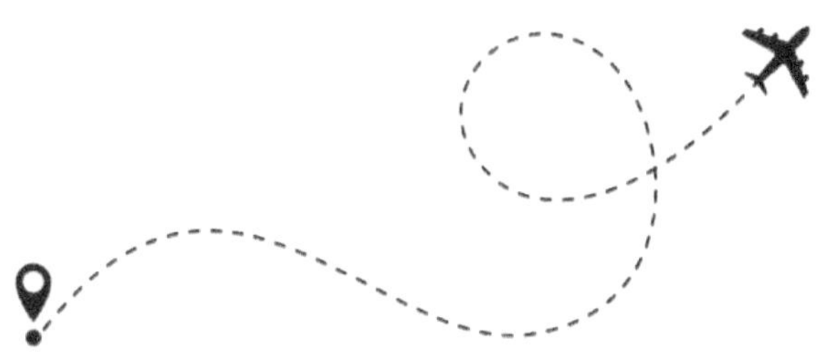

# Chapter One

Hello there! I'm Robbie, Robbie Wilson, an ordinary high school girl, with a not so ordinary story. I'm the same girl you'd collide with on your way to the cafeteria and not even apologise. I like to keep my distance from everyone, please stay away! The feeling that they know who I am just makes me so uncomfortable. I don't know why they try to get so close. I just don't like people. No one gets me, not even mom. Yea sure, maybe Ava gets me more than anybody else. Ava, she's my best friend, I love her. I spend most of my day with her, well, not most of my day but I still spend time with her more than I do with anyone else and I tell her everything.....well, almost. There are just some things I prefer taking to the grave. If I tell mom about it, she'd never believe me and rub it off. I'd just much rather sit in my room and read some case files listening to pop punk than go to the cool high school party at the popular rich kid's mansion whose parents are out of town. I like being alone, I mean, who wants to talk to Marcus, their "spoilt, socially active" classmate who can't even do 5 chin-ups without his lungs in his mouth!

Anyways, today, my second term of senior year started. I did arguably better than last year this time but I know I can do way better this term. After all, I need to get into a good university too. I'm thinking about what to study after school. I'm not really sure, though. I guess I'm more interested in psychology, law......criminal law maybe, I don't know. My counsellor at school, Ms. Johnson says I have the potential for it but I'll have to work really hard. I have a special passion for such subjects, it's so interesting to think about how the human brain works you know, especially for me. The criminal law part........I don't know, I watch serial killer documentaries often and I like to read about murders, killers and other crimes like that, it's actually very interesting. The other day, I read about this case where a woman murdered eight people from her family just so she could take away their fortune and run away! Although her ideas were good, she could've executed it in a much better way. Like, come on, why would you leave from the front door and take the family's car? Rookie mistake!

I had a very very tiring day today so I'll probably sleep early. Well, try to sleep atleast.

# Chapter Two

28th August 2018 9:03 AM

Good morning, I'm back! I'm writing this from the car because mom is dropping me off today. I told her I could walk but NO. She tries to hide it but she's actually just making up for leaving me alone with Jonah. Mom has some work conference so it's gonna be just Jonah and I at home and I have so much work to do, I don't know how I'll handle it. It's fine though, it'll be a good challenge for me and who knows, maybe I could have some fun with Jonah too! There's only one problem! Mom doesn't know....... Otherwise, she wouldn't have left me alone with Jonah. God, just thinking about it makes me feel like I'm on top of the Mount Everest or something. It gets so hard to breathe.

Anyway, we've reached and there's exactly 3 minutes left for school to start. In a rush mom, gotta go!

28th August 2018 2:56 PM

HELLO!

It's me again! School's finally over and now I have to go to drop mom to the airport. I decided to make plans with Ava to the fair nearby because I haven't done any socialising at all in the past month. I mean, I've probably spoken to my English teacher more than I have to anybody from my grade all year. So, Ava and I will have a great day out today and I have to reach back home before dark (obviously) and pick Jonah up, it's gonna be a hectic day.

• 4 •

# Chapter Three

28th August 2018 8:36 PM

I had a great day after so long, I actually enjoyed today so much. Ava and I had so much to eat and drink and then we rode the huge Ferris wheel which I was always scared to ride, we rode the rollercoasters, we ride every year together and it was just overall a fun day. Now, I'm home and I picked Jonah up from his friend's place. We're both home alone and I'm so nervous and scared. Phew, I'll go check what mom left us for dinner.

SHIT! SHIT! SHIT!

I just checked and mom forgot to make us dinner! There's no vegetables, no frozen food, nothing left in the fridge!

I take my phone, my hands trembling and scroll down worriedly waiting for the contact "Mom" to appear on the screen. Oh God, she's in her flight right now, she won't even reply!

I can't breathe, I'm panicking so much! My whole body shaking from head to toe. My vision blurred, I can't focus at all. I can't see what I'm typing, what is happening oh God! Okay, calm down Robbie, calm down!

*Robbie, it's fine, you'll find a solution just calm down!*

I take a deep breath and try to exhale all the stress out.

So, you're telling me, there's no food at home which means I have to get Jonah something to eat from the grocery store.

But what if I just don't?

No! No! I can't let that happen to Jonah, how will he go a whole night without food?

That leaves me with only one solution.

I have to go to the store at 9 p.m. and leave Jonah alone at home.

HOW ON EARTH WOULD I BE ABLE TO DO THAT!

SHITTTTTTTTTTTTTTTTTTTTTTTT!

HOW CAN I DO THAT WITH MY CONDITION!

............

I think it's time for you to know.

# Chapter Four

Okay!

I have a condition of sorts.

An issue.

I fear things, things that terrify me.

I have **foniasophobia.**

It's the constant fear of........getting murdered.

Yea, of course everybody's scared of death but I- I'm truly terrorised. I even match the symptoms!

I can't trust anyone because I don't even know who's a killer and who isn't.

I often think about death, I'm quite literally 'scared to death.'

I'm terrified.

I'm frightened.

I live in fear.

For me, every day is a challenge.

Because for me, there is only a fine line between *life* and *death*.

# Chapter Five

So, now that you know about all that, you probably realise how hard this is going to be for me.

Leaving my brother alone at home and walk to a store 10 minutes away at night.

For me, that's worse than a gun being put to an average person's head.

I've decided to do it. I've told Jonah not to open the door unless I call him on the landline and keep himself locked in his room. He doesn't know about my problem so he thinks it's weird that I'm reacting so much to this. Without more delay, I put on a black hoodie and pull up my hood as a shield from the world. I don't know, it's weird, but the hood makes me feel safer in a way. I take a cutter and put it in my pocket as a chill goes down my spine. I feel uneasy, I can feel something wrong in my bones but I must go on. My heartrate is over the roof right now and I'm sweating so much. I can't speak so I'm just doing everything in a hurry as I rush out of the house. I put the keys in my pocket and start walking out. I take a deep breath but I'm still shivering. I guess, death is inevitable. I mean, I had to face this sometime or the other, didn't I? I sigh and start walking down the lane and it's all going fine yet. I distinctly look around as I roll my eyeballs from left to right over my hood. Nothing. It's pitch dark and there's one streetlight like every 500 yards. A few more streetlights would have really helped...

At this point, I can feel the stress in my head. Okay, just two more minutes away. No cars passed by, no people either. I feel a little better and start walking calmly as my heartrate dips too. Suddenly I hear a loud engine roar around the corner and a car turns over the speed of 60 miles per hour with its headlights pointing straight at me as if to put a spotlight on me. I'm scared out of my mind. My heartrate, which was just going to go back to normal shoots up at a speed faster than light. I can't breathe at all. I start walking faster as I feel choked and the keys in my pocket cling against each other making the stinging sound of metal. The car moves past and at the same time, just as I start to calm down again, a person shows up from the opposite side.

OH!

OH MY GOD! OH MY GOD! OH MY GOD!

This might just be the end of me. My chest hurts now, I feel numb.

I walk even faster now as the person gets closer to me.

Shit! He's pacing towards me, I feel dizzy. He's coming closer. He's almost here. Oh my god, he's so close, does he have a knife with him? Is he here to kill me? I move my hand closer to my pocket with the cutter in it.

He passes by.

We cross ways and well, to say the least, I'm still alive. That's good, right? I calm down a little bit, walk the next few yards and then take off my hood to expose my untidy blonde hair in the bright streetlight hovering right over my head and I stop at the store.

Part 1: successful

Now, all I have to do is get some carrots, frozen pizza and milk.

# Chapter Six

I enter the door and the bell above rings. I stay still so I can come back to my senses and then walk up the lane to the fridge. I open the fridge and it makes a creaky sound. I turn around to see the old, stale cashier staring at me weirdly. I look away trying not to make eye contact as sweat trickles down my strands of hair. Frozen pizza, milk. Ah! All that's left now is the carrots. The carrots had to be at the polar opposite side of the shop too, didn't it? At this point, I'm annoyed and frustrated and scared and anxious and-

I'm overloaded with all sorts of emotions.

I take a deep sigh.

I just want to go home.

I start walking over to the other side and suddenly I hear a loud crash and a few screams. There was no one else in the shop when I came in, what? Where are these coming from? I feel butterflies in my stomach......but these butterflies are clawing away my insides trying to rip me open. Worried, I look over towards the counter

OH MY GOD!

OH MY GOD!

OH MY GOD!

OH MY GOD!

There are men wearing masks holding GUNS.

SHIT!

THEY HAVE GUNS!

THEY COULD KILL ME!

I'M GOING TO DIE TODAY!

ONE BULLET AND THAT'S IT, I'LL BE DEAD.

JESUS!

I try to get another glimpse at what's happening as my whole body shivers.

And then it kicks in.

I'm stuck in a robbery.

The two people take a look around as the last one holds a pistol up to the cashier's head.

No, no, I can't let him die.

He opens the drawer to give them the cash as they yell.

One of the guys suddenly turns towards where I am and I duck down.

I think he saw my head.

OH GOD! OH GOD! THEY'RE GONNA KILL ME!

I crawl over past the rows of cans, detergents, mints and chocolates back to the fridge area.

The man in the mask screams, "Who's there? Where are you hiding? You can't get out of here!'

NO! NO! NO! NO! NO!

I start hyperventilating. I feel nauseous and it's so hard to breathe.

I try to keep it down and breathe without making a sound.

The worst possible thing then takes place.

WHY AM I SO UNLUCKY?

My phone's illuminati ringtone suddenly starts echoing in the store.

NO! NO! NO! NO! NO!

The caller name says "Jonah". I can't help it. I have no option. My pulse rate shoots up as I rush to my pocket to turn it down. Half a ring is all that played but the robbers surely got a gist of where I was. The one who spotted me out shouts again and starts walking towards where I was....

# Chapter Seven

I look beside the shelves to see he was coming my way. I take a deep breath and now I have no option. I don't know how I'll do it or if I'll even be able to do it but here goes. It's now or never.

This is do or die.

I put my hand over to the pocket with the cutter and take it out. I slowly pull out the blade and duck to get into position. The man comes closer towards me.

How will I do this?

I can't do this.

NO!

I won't be able to do it.

I can't do it!

I can't do it!

As my vision starts to focus and a ringing sound exits my ears, "HERE!" I hear a loud scream from a man right on top of my head as I impulsively dodge to the side and stick the blade into his leg.

Everything is happening so quickly, I can't register it. I have no idea what's happening. The man disarmed, I take his gun, run towards the other rows of shelves and look over the counter. One of them just shot a bullet.

SHIT!

I'm dying.

I'm dying today.

I can't do this.

I can't do this.

I can't do this.

Okay! No!

I HAVE to do this!

For Jonah.

FOR JONAH!

I look over the shelf, see the two men and leap to point my gun up and empty the mag in their bodies. I'm guessing I don't have good aim but they were both bleeding and disarmed so that was enough.

I fall.

Phew!

I fall on my knees as it feels like my body itself is disowning me. Sobbing, crying, and screaming at a frequency I didn't even know I had in me. This was real pain. I thought I knew how pain felt but, I guess I was wrong because nothing I'd ever done felt as hurtful as this did. A faint voice in my head cursed me every moment as I felt afraid, I don't know why it's not like I did anything wrong, but I felt perplexed. It seemed like the world had just rewritten itself, like I was just born again with no knowledge of this cruel, unjust world.

I go check if the cashier is okay and call 911 on my phone.

It was then that I realised.....

I had just murdered someone.

A girl who has a phobia of getting killed had just killed someone.

# Chapter Eight

Okay Robbie, calm down! You did what you had to. You saved your life. This is all for Jonah. All just for your little bro. I try to calm myself down as I take out my phone with my trembling hands. I swipe to the recent calls list and click on 'Jonah'.

"H-he-hey Jonah. Jonah, are you okay? Jonah, are you good? Stay where you are Jonah, I'll be right there! You didn't open the door, right?"

He said he was okay and told me to calm down....how could I calm down right now when I'd practically witnessed the worst nightmare of my life? I told him I'd be there in 10 minutes.

I still can't breathe properly. My tears aren't stopping.

Suddenly, I hear the ring of a police alarm. A sense of relief goes through me as I stand up and walk outside the store with the gun in my hand and the food. The police look towards me and two officers come and ask me a few questions. I give them the gun, told them everything about what happened and run back home faster than I'd run on junior school sports day. Oh god, I hate this. Why me?! Ugh, I'm annoyed. I feel everything and nothing at the same time. I'm taking one breath every five seconds. I'm sweating, shivering, my whole body hurts and I'm so nauseous. I don't know what but something in my stomach is dancing around oh no-

I think I just took out everything I've eaten in the last one month but at least I feel better. Pieces of cereal I ate for breakfast, the salami I ate today, it's all there. It's gooey and pink and yellow with chunks in between, something about the colour is very off, and it's such a mess. I can smell a mix of pizza, digested vegetables and the stink of three day old chicken. Now, to think that a pigeon will feed on my sprayed out guts or some poor guy will have to clean this off the side walk. GOD! I'M DISGUSTING! This stinks, maybe I should stop staring at my vomit and go home...

I rush back home, open the door, close it faster than a squirrel running back to its burrow and just stand behind the door. I take a minute to process everything that happened along with a few deep breaths. I run over to the room that Jonah is in, open the door with a bang and see Jonah still there intact just playing a game on his computer. Oh lord, I feel so relieved, I just go and hug him tightly for a whole minute.

"I love you, Jonah, you know that right?"

He nods and smiles back warmly.

I hand him the carrots and milk.

"Come to the kitchen, we'll make you pizza."

He snatches the pizza from me, runs ahead of me to the kitchen and starts microwaving the pizza.

He looks at me with his usual cheeky smile and fresh dimples, "Thank you, Robbie!" and that's when I knew it was all worth it.

# Chapter Nine

We eat the pizza, well, mostly Jonah because I didn't feel like it and we go back to our room. I freshen up, change into my nightwear and go to my table. I sit and think about everything that happened and type it out on a word document along with how I felt. I like writing, it's what I'm most passionate about. That's why I'm writing this journal, and why else would I actually be using proper punctuation and capitalisation, I'm an American high schooler, do you really expect that? That's also why I have a blog, I blog about my phobia and how I deal with it, to help others facing the same issue. Of course, I keep my identity anonymous though. My blog is called 'The game of death'. I upload my write up titled 'Death is Inevitable' as a draft and decide to work on the rest later. "Jonah, Let's go to sleep now!"

Today was an exhausting day to say the least, I'm dead tired, physically and mentally both. I throw myself on the bed and lie down in a comfortable position. I feel less stressed for now, I close my eyes and drift down into the darkness of my thoughts. From the robbery to the time we went to Bali with mom, I visit the whole dark world with my thoughts in only 60 minutes, and then I finally go to sleep. Good night! The next second I open my eyes I'm at- oh no!...NO! NO! NO! NOT THIS PLEASE! ANYTHING BUT THIS! I'm here, sitting in a first class seat heading towards Australia for a holiday with a soda can in my hands. I look through the rows of seats and see a well-built man in a navy blue jacket lined with gold badges and medals and blue trousers wearing a cap with a gold logo of the air force. It's dad......

# Chapter Ten

Dad's an air marshal. He just got off his previous flight on duty and boarded with us so he's in uniform. I guess he's working this flight too then. Officially, he isn't on duty but you know how dad is. I look at him and laugh as he mocks me. I'm on the aisle seat. Casually sipping on my soda, I hear some chaos towards the back of the plane. I look towards dad and he has a peculiar expression. He starts walking over to the backside until suddenly, a few yells shake the plane, quite literally. A bearded man pushes through the dividers and comes to our half of the plane. OH NO! WHAT!

He has a gun in his hands. An actual full size AK. My hands start trembling and I drop the soda on the floor with a crash. Dad looks at me and I look at him with my mouth wide open, eyebrows high and eyes that showed nothing but fear. Our flight had been hijacked. I'm sweating, panicking with no idea what to do. Dad shows me a thumbs up sign and mouths "It'll be okay, I'm here for you." He walks up to the terrorist.

"Aye, don't move, what do you think you're doing?"

Dad with his hands up says, "I'm an air marshal for the US air force, sir. Don't worry I just want to talk, I don't intend to hurt you, if you would please put your gun down." At this moment suddenly, another man pushes through and starts yelling in a language that sounded rather aggressive. He pushes my dad and grabs him by the collar. I feel choked, my hand over my mouth because otherwise my sobs would be too loud. My heart skipping a beat every time one of the men yelled. I hide behind a seat. NO, NO, NO! I can't let anything happen to dad. How will I survive without dad? He's the only one who gets me! It's fine, dad knows his job, he can handle this, right?

I look over at mom and Jonah. They're both in a situation almost as bad as mine. Mom has Jonah tugged under her arms while she tries hard to keep herself stable. Grabbing my attention, I hear a bullet fire. My heart practically stops beating as I rapidly turn around. A sigh of relief passes through me, it wasn't dad. He's still trying to convince the hijackers. "What do you want? We're ready to meet all your demands, just tell us how much money you want!" The man, who seemed rather crazy, used his gun to smack dad in his torso. My shrieking cries tore through my throat trying to escape the barriers made by my hand. I get up from my seat trying to hold in the anger. I start walking towards the terrorists until dad sees me and screams, "Robbie, no! It's not worth it! Go back!" My chest pained, it felt numb and at the same time it felt like a 100 needles surrounded me just a few centimetres away from my body, but they won't touch just yet. I can't move, I'm stuck, It's like I can feel the pain without being in pain, but I go back to my seat. Looking back, I see dad struggling, resisting, just trying to find a solution. One of the men said, "Leave him for now! He's had enough, we might need him later as a hostage." The other agreed and started patrolling along the narrow passage of the flight. Just as the men turned away, my dad took out a satellite phone from his pocket and dialled a number. He lifted his heavy body up with much effort as he bled from his nose and a part of his pants ripped. He walked through the divider curtain to where the terrorist was and said into his radio, "P11-034 speaking, it's a squawk 7500, I repea-". A striking sound of a bullet firing echoed through the flight as I saw dad's body dropping spilled with blood. A hole in the middle of his torso, his face getting pale, blood dripping out continuously and his wound dark red, as if the blood from inside couldn't wait to escape this prison. Those once passionate, powerful, and understanding eyes that showed paradise, now looked like that magic had been sucked straight out of them.

I scream at the top of my lungs, sobbing, screeching, crying, when I open my eyes.

It was a nightmare.

I take a deep sigh of reassurance and check the time on my watch, 6:30 AM.

Phew. Yep, that's how my dad passed away, or at least how my brain imagines it. When I was on that flight, all I saw was his body falling through the curtains and heard the bullet. I didn't know what had happened behind the curtains, or how his body looked like after death. All I knew was that the one person whom I trusted most was no longer with me. I love dad. He's the only one I told about my problem. He's the only one who understood, and tried to help with me it. That day tore me apart, it broke me inside. My mom was beside me, and so was my brother, but they didn't know why I was hiding behind that seat, all that I could see was the only one who truly felt my pain was going away from me. I was losing him, forever. The incident is probably what triggered my phobia more. I felt unsafe, I had no one to talk to my problem about. But I knew dad would be with me, listening to my problems from somewhere and being there for me. I loved him. I still do, I love you dad. If only he was here.

# Chapter Eleven

Okay, that was a lot for a day but at least mom's going to be back today so that's something positive after so long. I don't even know if I want to attend school today but I have my exams coming up soon and I don't want to fail the semester so I should probably go. I mean, yeah it's been a hard day and night but eh, I'll push through. I still haven't processed anything that happened, I'm in for a long day. Plus I get to talk to Ms. Johnson, so that's cool, right?

I wake Jonah up, tell him to get ready and freshen up. I go into the bathroom to brush my teeth when I look up to the mirror lined with silver crystals on the side. I don't recognise who I am anymore. I hate who I've become. Like, look at me, from the mysterious introvert with neatly tied hair to this worried, unsure *killer* who's tanned and filled with pimples and dark circles on her face now. I pour some face wash on my hand and aggressively scrub my face. Still the same. Huh, I guess it's just side effects of the great events of the last 2 days, yay!

I take a quick shower, put on my black jeans and dark grey hoodie and take out some cereal from the kitchen.

"Jonah, quick!"

"Coming," he screams from his room.

I serve both of us some cereal and it's time for us to leave.

I drop Jonah off at his friend's house and then wait outside Ava's.

Why isn't she here yet? It's already five minutes later than the usual time.

Ava walks out of her teakwood finished door in a colourful outfit and her dark skin.

"Hey Girl!" she says as she comes and high fives me.

"Hi Ava!" I reply back.

"What's wrong, you look off today?" she calls me out like how does she see it already????

"Eh, nothing just couldn't sleep well last night," I say as if my life was going completely ordinarily and everything was totally normal.

God, I feel bad about hiding it from her. I still haven't told her about the phobia.

AND YOU KNOW WHAT........

I CAN'T TAKE IT ANYMORE........

I'm not the tough mysterious girl everyone thinks I am.

I'm done pretending everything around me is fine, that I'm fine.

Because the truth is I'M NOT!

I'M NOT FINE!

I have all of this frustration, this anger, built up inside me and I don't have anyone to talk to about it. I can't share anything with anybody because Mom is just too busy with work and Dad's gone and I hate this sooooo much.

AAAAAAAAAAAAARRRGGGHHHHHHHHHHHHHH!

And it's not that I don't want to tell Ava because I'm all strong and mentally set. NO!

I don't even know what's going on in my head.

I can't keep track of anything.

I don't want to tell Ava because she's the only one I have anymore.

And if I tell her about my issue, she'll start pitying me and act like everything I do and say is right

JUST BECAUSE I HAVE A PROBLEM!

NO! EW GOD! NO!

I absolutely despise pity.

I can't take this and I-

"Robbie............Robbie, what's happening? Are you okay?" says Ava as she shakes my body to get me to my senses.

Oh shit! That was very bad timing for a breakdown.

"Yea, yea, I'm fine just a lot of school stress lately," I reply as I shrug the topic off.

We reach school and we go separate ways to our classes.

First class today is life skills and we're talking about the value of one's life and what's really right or wrong.

just- perfect-

# Chapter Twelve

My head is aching and this conversation is making me feel really dizzy. I decide to go to the medical room and get an Aspirin. I come back and the first sentence I hear is, "Death is a blessing in disguise"

Ouch! I feel a sting towards the back of my head as I walk back to my desk. I sit down with my head down listening to the conversations only distinctly. I fall half asleep trying not to pay attention in class. I hear the 'ding' sound of the clock and the class is finally over.

The rest of the day just goes by and I can't stop thinking about everything that's happened.

Okay, I need to talk to someone about this desperately so I've decided to tell Ms. Johnson.

I walk up to her cabin and knock.

"Who is it?"

"It's me Miss, Robbie"

"Come in."

I open the door handle as the hinges creak and I enter her office. A small cozy room made out of mainly dark oak wood with marble décor and a small table with her computer, cup of coffee, a pencil stand and a lighter. Her cabin makes me feel at home. I sit on the rolling chair and put down my bag.

"So, tell me what's up"

"Ms. Johnson, I've been wanting to tell you something for quite some time now and I just needed to tell someone now that dad's gone and everything-"

I start lightly sobbing now, all the built up emotion pouring out.

"Hey, hey, hey come on Robbie! There's no need to cry, it's alright, I'm there for you. You can always tell me anything you know that right?" she interrupts me as she hands me a tissue.

I wipe my nose off and take a deep breath to calm down.

"Miss, it's just that- I just- I have a problem."

"Go ahead, I'm all ears, I got you."

I sigh.

"I have a phobia of sorts. Foniasophobia."

She looks at me with watery eyes and a genuinely concerned face. No pity. Thank god!

"Oh sweetie," she says as she gets up from her chair to hug me, "It's alright. I'll help you with all that I can, tell me more about it."

I tell her about everything- dad, my blog, the nightmare.........well, everything but the robbery.

"Robbie, I know this is the last thing you want to hear right now but would you please try to visit a psychologist? Not much just once a week but it'll really help you Robbie, I promise," she says convincingly.

"No, no, no, oh god no, how would therapy help me in any way, Miss? The issue isn't even diagnosable," I tell her without any sign of agreement even though I might've thought about it myself before. I guess I was just trying to fool myself.

"Think about it, Robbie. You have a trained professional to share things with. If not much, at least you can talk openly and get proper advice."

"Mom would never agree to pay me for it," I say protesting.

"Worth a try, Robbie," she takes a slight pause, "Robbie, you're dying, I can see it in your eyes, you're perfectly fit physically, but inside, mentally you're slowly and slowly ebbing away. You've lost all hope, Robbie."

I look down disappointed in myself, she was right. I had lost hope after all it's not like anything hopeful ever happened with me after dad left.

I sigh and agree, "Alright, I'll try asking mom when she's back tonight."

I stand up and start to exit the room, "Bye, Miss Johnson!"

"Bye!" she replies.

I'm almost out when I look back and say, "Thank you Miss, really, for everything!"

She laughs cheerfully and smiles at me, "Don't worry about it."

# Chapter Thirteen

I pick Jonah up from day-care and go back home. I freshen up, go to my room and start writing about everything that's happened. I completely forgot to blog about it. I play some pop punk and fall into the pit of my thoughts yet again.

WHAT???!!!

I just spent three hours writing without realising and mom's going to be back in 30 minutes and I'm not prepared for anything. I don't know how I'll ask her. Will I be able to do it? I start freaking out.

At least, I finished my post. I've called this one, '*death: a blessing in disguise?*'. Yep, you guessed it, inspired by the random classmate who said that today morning. Thanks for an awesome title!

I close my computer, stuff back my headphones and notebook into their drawers and take out my bio textbook. Amidst all this, I completely forgot my exams start next week. Life is such a task, ugh.

Mom's back home. She just came back and right now she's gone into her room to change. I got this, I'm ready. Mom comes out and walks into the kitchen. I sit in the living room and call her. She comes and sits on the sofa next to me.

"Yeah, what happened honey?" she checks on me.

"What didn't?" I whisper under my breath

Ahem!

"Mom, can I tell you something?"

"Sure," she starts getting curious.

"Mom, I need some money.......to visit a psychologist." She chuckles.

"Honey why do you need a psychologist? You teenagers nowadays!"

"No mom, I talked to Ms. Johnson today...I NEED HELP!"

"Help with what Robbie??"

"I-...mom...stress, I'm stressed, school work, people...I'M JUST STRESSED!" I say hesitantly.

"Robbie, psychologists won't help you with anything. They are all fake...a way to capitalize off children without enough support. They can't help you with your stress, I can help you, and you can help yourself."

"Mom...mom I just...please...I need this"

My eyes start tearing up.

"ROBBIE-?" Mom raises her tone, it was maybe because she was concerned, but that was enough to trigger me, along with my tucked in emotions of course.

I burst out in tears.

"WHAT KIND OF MOTHER ARE YOU?...YOUR CHILD NEEDS HELP...WHY WON'T YOU HELP ME?"

I hurt mom. I could see it on her face. She collapses on a chair beside her and starts sobbing, "I WANT TO HELP YOU...TRUST ME ROBBIE, I LOVE YOU!...but I can't, not after your dad..." she sniffs and tries to control herself, "I can't afford a psychiatrist Robbie, I wish I could but it's been hard after Dave...you know."

I'm stunned, my eyes wide open, filled with tears and despair, I get up and hug mom tightly, it helped...helped the both of us. I don't want to make her feel worse, I DON'T WANT TO FEEL WORSE. We stay there for a long 5 minutes and then I apologise for screaming at her.

"No Robbie, don't apologise, I'm sorry...I really am. Maybe Ms. Johnson can help you"

"Yes mom I'll talk to her."

"Robbie," she calls out, "I love you."

I smile, "I love you too mom."

# Chapter Fourteen

I wake up an hour before I usually do since I slept a bit too early yesterday. It's just 6. I think I should study because exams are right around the corner. Just before that I check my blog. 140 likes and only 60 comments on the latest post. That could've done so much better. I study for a few minutes, take a shower and leave for school. I walk to school with Ava like the usual and sleep through school. Finally, its recess and I can go meet Ms. Johnson.

I take a deep breath and walk up to her door. I knock the door but there's no response. I wait for another 10 minutes outside her door. Nothing.

Why am I so unlucky?????????

I go back to class and stare at the clock waiting for the day to somehow pass by.

AP Bio, AP Literature, Psychology and finally the day's over.

I hurriedly stuff everything in my bag and rush to Ms. Johnson's office.

*Knock, knock*

"Come in"

YES!

A voice from inside me finally brings a spark of hope in me.....until I realise what I was going to tell her.

"Hey Robbie" she says.

"Hi Miss" I reply.

"so........" she asks expectantly.

I shake my head.

"Mom didn't agree. She said we can't afford it after dad...," I tell her, disappointed.

She sighs and sits back on her chair. She doesn't say a word for another 3 minutes with her hand lightly stroking her chin as if she was thinking of something. And then suddenly, I see a smile lighting up her face. My heart rate rises in excitement. She's definitely up to something.

She says excitedly, "Okay Robbie, listen carefully alright. Will you be willing to go visit a friend of mine who's a renowned psychologist once a week for free?"

OH MY GOD!

Joy spreads around my face as I open my mouth wide in shock. I start laughing and nod.

Ms. Johnson picks up her phone from the table and dials a number.

After about three rings the person on the other side picks up.

I can hear only what Ms. Johnson says.

"Hey............I need a favour.............yeah, yeah she's very close to me.........yea, no, there is definitely an issue there.........please         it's         a         sincere request......hmmmmm........yes, okay, Wednesdays 4 p.m. you got that.....Thanks, Bye!"

Ms. Johnson shows some victory signs and puts down her phone. I laugh out loud and go and hug her.

"Thank you so much Miss, you're the best," I say as I hug her even tighter. The frown on my face was now overtaken by a fresh smile. I looked toward my watch- what day was it today?

Wednesday.

What's the time?

3.45!

I look towards Ms. Johnson and smile, "Gotta go Miss, I have a therapy session to go to!"

She smiles back and sends a flying kiss right at me as I leave her room running across the footpath in enthusiasm towards Dr. Shah's clinic.

# Chapter Fifteen

I get out of the lift and I see a giant pinkish board with bold purple text on it saying *'Dr. Shah's Clinic'*

From the moment I read it to the moment I pushed open the door handle, I had gone from being happy to excited to nervous to scared and finally just ready for it. I push open the long door handle and see an Indian woman sitting on a rolling chair on the phone with someone. She wore a peculiar serious expression that somehow made you laugh. Her office was two sofas put up facing each other, a dark oak table with a computer and two chairs on either side, and the rest of the room was really just an aesthetic. Bookshelves piled up with vibrant coloured spines and showpieces of different movie characters lined the walls. I don't know how this happened but even though I had reached here just a few seconds ago, I felt comfortable, it felt like I was safe. I go and stand beside the table waiting for her to get off the phone. "Hiii! You must be Robbie?" she says as she puts down the phone. Okay, I did not expect her to sound like that at all. Her voice is pleasant and high pitched in a good way, almost dreamy, completely in contrast with the serious look on her face. The room smells like coffee mixed with the scent of lavender.

"Yep, that's me. Robbie, Robbie Wilson. Nice to meet you Dr.................? Shah?"

She lets out a little cheerful laugh that lightens up the atmosphere.

"Call me Sophie. Short for Sofia," she instructs.

I have a weird expression on my face because the name is rather uncommon.

"Yea, I know, it's weird. My parents are from India but I was born here which is why the name. Long story," she laughs it off.

Damn, I thought I'd kept it low-key.

I'm starting to see what she's all about. Maybe this'll go better than I expected it to.

"Anyway, take a seat Robbie. You're in for a ride!" she says.

I sit on the green sofa and put my bag down.

We introduce ourselves followed by some small talk and then the real deal.

"So, what's the problem, Robbie?" she asks me.

"I think I have Foniasophobia. I felt the fear when I was young but thought it was just normal until it started happening very often. I googled up the symptoms and almost all of them matched. And then, with dad's death, it all just- yeah," I sigh.

"It's alright Robbie. Now that you've got therapy, it's going to help you a lot. Even though the issue isn't diagnosable, let's start with a few questions, okay?"

"Sure" I reply.

The next 40 minutes or so just speed past as she asks me questions and we talk about everything that's happened with me. Again, I didn't have the will to tell her about the robbery yet so eh, I guess I'll tell her later. No biggie.

The session ends and she concludes, "Okay, so Robbie, yes, you might have Foniasophobia. Although we can't confirm anything, your symptoms agree with us. For now, let's just continue the anti-anxiety exercises I told you and we don't need any medication. You did well today. Remember, next Wednesday, 4 p.m. again."

She smiles at me.

I look back and say, "Thanks Doc, Bye!"

# Chapter Sixteen

It's exam time soon. I'm spending all day and night studying, I have no time to get distracted. I have no time for anything, except Dr. Shah's clinic once a week obviously and an hour of free time in the day. I told mom I visit Dr. Shah for free because Ms. Johnson thought I really needed it because of "exam pressure" and "career stress".

Heh! Sure!

She wasn't very happy about it but I guess she didn't mind it too much either because she let me go. My days are very stagnant for now. I go to school, come back home, group study with Ava, read a few case files or watch a few crime documentaries and go back to studying. I can't wait for the next therapy session. I even have to tell Doc about the robbery. The next few days just pass by without anything much happening.

*4 days later*

I have an exam tomorrow morning and I'm not confident at all. It's psychology though so I'll get through. I should get a good night's sleep so I'll probably stop studying now. I lie on the bed and make sure Jonah's asleep. Weird thoughts cross my mind as usual and it takes me an hour to sleep.

'What if someone murders Jonah while I'm asleep?'

'No one's making sure he's okay'

'I have to take care of him.'

Hmm, I have my psychology exam tomorrow, I'm nervous, sweat trickling down my back, I imagine how the exam will go, have I prepared enough? Will that happen again? These imaginations turn into slight hallucinations. I imagine myself in the class, I'm getting a panic attack, and I freak out. The hallucinations turn into nightmares- I blank out in the exam. The flashbacks happen again, the dark thoughts infiltrate my mind and now suddenly, I have a gun in my hand. WHAT IS HAPPENING? The next thing I see, my teacher on the floor, blood pouring from his lifeless body, a hole right in the middle of his torso.

I'm shivering as I suddenly wake up with a jerk. I pant as I look towards Jonah to make sure he's okay. I take my phone from my side table and enter the washroom. My heart goes faster and faster as hot flushes go through my body. I check the time, 3.36 AM. I sit on a stool and try to come back to my senses. I take long deep breaths and calm down a little. I start crying and shrieking. I'm pissed off right now. I have an exam tomorrow, how am I going to do this? I burst into tears and sob as I wash my nose every 5 minutes. I calm down after an hour and come out of the washroom.

There's no one there. It's safe. I go back to my bed and pull my blanket up to my nose. Just 2 and a half hours before I wake up. Goodnight again!

# Chapter Seventeen

It's exam day today. I wake up, get ready and have breakfast, the usual. I walk up to Ava's house as she comes out holding a 400 page textbook open in her hand that was so thick it could be used as a brick in her house. I look at her and laugh and we start walking. Just as we reach school, the entrance is chaotic. People crashing bikes, rampaging through the doors, bashing into lockers. Yep, that's when you know it's exam day. I walk up to my exam room and sit on the seat that reads *Robbie Wilson*. I take out my textbook and revise until our invigilator walks in. A man who looks like he's in his mid- 30s with curly brown hair who's wearing brown trousers, a white checkered shirt, a blue jacket and a red tie.

"Books in, bags away, 5 minutes left for reading time everybody!" he says loudly.

I put my book in and take my bag to the front of the class. I get handed the question paper as I skim through it. The 15 minutes of reading time just swoosh away and I get handed the answer sheet. I put my pen on the paper and write my details. Just as I write '*Ans 1*', my brain blanks out. It's all coming back. Everything from last night, the nightmare, leading me to dad's death..............the robbery.

NO!

Not the robbery right now, please, no!

'I killed people, I murdered them with my own hands. What if they had a children, a family? What if they were helpless to do such acts? What if I was the wrong one here?'

These thoughts start taking over my mind as I lose full focus.

NO, I WON'T LET THIS HAPPEN, NOT TODAY.

I shake my head and get back in control. I start writing the answers as my pen automatically slides over the sheet.

"Robbie, is everything alright?" the teacher asks looking at me.

Still in a state of panic, "Yea, just didn't get good sleep last night."

I start sweating.

'Your dad got killed in front of your eyes and you couldn't do anything'

They're coming again.

NO!

I shut my mind off and stop myself from getting distracted. The next two hours were just a battle between me and my mind.

Okay, so that got done somehow and I can NEVER let that happen again. I almost messed up the whole semester for myself. My college, my career, my whole life, it was all at stake. Oh god, I just realised. I have Literature on Thursday, my worst subject. I have to miss therapy, I have no other option.

The next few days just pass by like a moment in time. I think I didn't fail the semester, at least I hope so and I have therapy at 4 p.m. today. I've also decided to do criminal law with psychology for college. I'm excited for today. Finally, I can meet Doc after so many days.

# Chapter Eighteen

I walk down the alley to Doc's clinic again. The same pink board but this time instead of nervousness, pure joy took over me. I love coming here in just a few visits. I enter the clinic and wave to Doc.

"Hey Robbie, how's it going?"

"Nothing much Doc, just got done with exams and I have loads of things to tell you."
"Alright then, what are we waiting for?"

I tell her about the hallucinations, exam incidents and then finally, the robbery.

"And there's another thing which I forgot to tell you about. I was forced into an incident some time ago." I tell her hesitantly.

"What do you mean, what 'incident'?"

"I went to the local store at night and got stuck in an armed robbery," I tell her.

"Oh god, that must've been horrifying Robbie. How did you feel?" she asks.

"Yeah, I was really scared but then I killed them. I killed them all," I say with a slight smirk on my face.

"What?! You killed the robbers?" she asks in astonishment.

"Yeah, I mean, I had to protect myself and the shopkeeper, you know?" I shrug it off.

"WHAT??" she yells in shock, "AND YOU'RE TELLING ME THIS NOW??? ROBBIE, DO YOU HAVE ANY IDEA HOW IMPORTANT THIS IS?"

I think Doc sees my reaction and immediately calms down.

"Sorry about the tone. I panicked," she takes a breath, "Do you know how much this can affect the situation, Robbie? This was such an important detail, why haven't you told me this yet? Is there anything else you haven't told me?" Sophie seems a bit worried.

"Nothing important, no, I don't think so," I answer.

"Robbie, this isn't just your thoughts anymore, it's the real world. You've killed three human beings, there's going to be actions, legal procedures. You can't let what's troubling you from the inside guide your actions on the outside. This is the real world, no matter what problem you have, no one's as understanding as the people who care about you. *You can't harm a person, Robbie. No matter what.*" She asks me a few more questions and then has a concerned expression on her face.

I try to hide back my tears, "I'm sorry. I had no choice."

"I know, Robbie, you're a good child. Just don't let your emotions take control of you. And remember, I'll always be there for you."

I smile at her and nod.

"Robbie, I'm going to be honest with you right now. I think Foniasophobia might not be the root to your problems anymore. You might be dealing with something completely different here. We call it Harm OCD, are you aware of what that is? "

"Uh, no. What is it Doc? Is it serious?" I start feeling impatient.

"Don't worry. It's very common among people who've been through something like you have," she sighs, "Imagine Foniasophobia is 2-dimensional."

"2-dimensional? Huh?" I say, confused.

"Foniasophobia is the fear of getting killed, 2d........ Harm OCD is a little more complex.....3 dimensional. Imagine a rat, caught in a trap. The first instinct it has, is to gnaw off its own leg. Even though losing a leg might make it difficult for the rat to survive, it's willing to harm itself to escape the trap just for temporary satisfaction. Robbie, you might experience some violent instincts.......some impulsive and aggressive behaviour which you might feel goes exactly against your Foniasophobia. Everything that you earlier feared, you will now crave," she explains.

"Doc, what are you trying to say?" I feel really lost now.

"Robbie, you might have some violent thoughts. Thoughts that you know are bad for you but will still attract you. It's like a cigarette, the more you try to stay away from it, the more you want it," she elaborates.

"WHAT ARE YOU TRYING TO SAY? I'M A MURDERER?!" I freak out.

"No, not at all Robbie. Just remember that if you ever have any such thoughts, try to look back. Think of the better times, you've pushed through this far. You got to keep going Robbie, life isn't easy so just hold on. And I'll always support you. You have your mother, your brother, maybe try sharing with a trusted friend? You aren't alone in this Robbie and you never will be," she tries to comfort me.

I can't breathe. I think someone just sucked my life out of me. It's like I paused in a moment in time. I can't move, I feel numb. I'm hyperventilating. Everything looks like its rotating and I feel like I want to vomit.

"So I'm going to get thoughts about murder?" I take a pause, "but-but it can't be, like yea I killed 3 people but that's just cause I was defending myself right? I would've died Doc." I burst into tears and start shrieking under my breath. Sophie comes towards me and hugs me as I try hard to stop my tears. I sniff and wipe my nose with a tissue.

"It's not your fault, Robbie, it'll be fine. And for a little extreme cases, I'll give you some pills. Promise me, you'll have them only in emergencies. In no possible way, and I mean never Robbie, do I want you to be dependent on them. They're highly drug-intensive pills, intake should be very very very limited. Be careful with them. See you next week and call me if you need something!"

I look down in misery, feeling depressed and start walking home.

# Chapter Nineteen

Wow, that was a lot to handle. What's wrong with me? What have I done to let this happen? What if I hurt someone? What if I can't stop myself from hurting someone?

All these thoughts lingering in my mind exhaust me to a point that I force myself to calm down.

Okay, it's alright. Doc said I can get through this and I will. I feel way calmer by the time I reach home. I can't tell anybody about this though. How will they react? What if they stop talking to me? AND-

OH GOD! THE WORST!

What if they start pitying me?

I won't tell anybody about the OCD and the pills. If mom finds out about the pills, I'm dead. I'll keep it in the bottom drawer of my bed side table, mom never checks that. And I'll keep one pack in my bag and one in my pocket for emergencies. Yes, perfect. Do I want to write about it on my blog? Eh, sure, I guess. I have all summer break just to blog and prepare for law school anyways so I'm pretty much free.

*summer break ends*

Hello again. As it turns out, I wasted all summer break researching and blogging about murders. Well, the time isn't really "wasted" anymore because that's study for me. Remember, criminal law? So what I used to do as a fun activity is now the same thing I study and give exams for. Damn, that's actually very cool. Today's my first day of law school and I'm actually pretty confident. I mean I'm probably more researched than everybody else in general anyways. I leave home and mom drives me to college today. I enter and walk past the beige painted halls into my class that was filled with students everywhere. In the front, was a big projector and the rest was filled with seats. I go and choose a seat I like that wasn't too close to the front. A few minutes later, a man wearing a dark blue collared t-shirt and black jeans enters. He picks up a laser pointer and starts pointing towards the board after putting on a PowerPoint. He gets in to the class and speaks oddly quickly, as if he's in a rush, "Good morning class. I'll be your criminal law teacher. Let's not waste any time on intros and get straight to the topic. Today, we'll be studying about first degree murders and how to prove someone guilty. Read this situation and tell me the possibilities within the next 30 seconds."

WHAT!

30 seconds only?????? Is this guy crazy????

I almost finish reading through the situation when I hear a loud echo, "Alright, that's it. Tell me what you got." I see hands raising, the hands gradually increasing.

"Sir, the assistant could've poisoned the coffee."

"Not possible, the assistant was on CCTV throughout, next."

"Sir, suicide? He could've taken poison himself. Possible reasons- stress, workload, personal issues, even his business wasn't doing very well at the time."

"Ahhhh, he died mid-day when he'd been at work all day. Most poisons start showing effects in just a few minutes, couldn't have been the case NEXT!"

"Sir, he got a vaccination right the day before. Maybe something else was in the injection."

"Again, too much of a time margin. Effects would've started before. Next!"

Another 40 or so people give their takes until it's almost the end of the lesson. I make eye contact with the teacher. I think eagerly but I have nothing. Absolutely nothing.

"You, the one at the back in the grey hoodie, you got something?" he looks at me.

I feel hassled because I've thought about this so much..........but then suddenly IT HITS.

I imagine myself in the situation. If I'm the killer, what would I do? Poison a food item? Nah, too amateur, will leave very less suspects. Air vent infiltration? Nope, getting in is very hard without being spotted by a camera. Hmmm, what would I do? What would you do, Robbie? Think quick. How would I murder this man? How can I poison him...............WAIT, THAT'S IT! Poisoning can be very open and lead to suspicions so I would use poison as a fake. I would murder him when he goes away from his office. I'd hide at the rooftop where he goes to smoke a cigarette and attack him just when he's at his least guard. Pounce from the back, cover his mouth with a cloth, choke him to his death and put poison over his mouth as a distraction. A flawless murder plan. THAT'S IT!

"Sir, the poison was just a cover up. There's a buffer of 20 minutes when he goes to the roof to smoke a cigarette. The body was found at the rooftop and there are no forensics reports that verify the poison so it isn't necessary he died to the poison," I say nervously.

The class is silent. Pin drop silence.

The teacher is staring into my soul to a point that I want to break eye contact. His face lights up a little and he starts clapping slowly.

"Robbie. Robbie Wilson, right?"

I nod.

"Class, can we have a round of applause for Robbie?"

Everybody applauds, I feel good but something feels wrong. I'm proud of myself, but I realise I'm not really proud of figuring out the task. I'm proud of murdering a man. Even if it was in my imagination. Killing a person, it just makes me feel like nothing else does, the thrill, the adrenaline rush, it's like a game for me.

"That's it for today, class," he looks at me, "Well done, Robbie!"

Damn, that was a good first class!

# Chapter Twenty

I walk to the cafeteria and even though that went perfectly, something feels odd at the back of my head. I go and sit at a table, isolated, away from the main crowd. I was happily eating my salami sandwich when my head started hurting again. Then, this guy, almost 5 feet 10' with light skin and childish eyes comes up and asks me if he could sit there.

Already irritated, I say, "I'd rather sit alone, if you don't mind."

He seemed helpless and said, "Actually, I couldn't find any other seat so I thought I could sit here."

The sting at the back of my head increasing, "I SAID I WANT TO SIT ALONE, DON'T YOU GET IT?" I almost yelled.

God, what's happening to me? What's going on in my head? I start heading back home and take out two pills from my pocket as quickly as I could. I reach my room and just sit there and breathe for about 15 minutes. The pills really help, this feels good. I calm myself down and read a few more case files. Eh, it's probably the stress of the first day so I sleep early. I wake up the next day with a fresher mind but there's still that little feeling in my head. Oh, I just remembered. I haven't told Ava about anything yet. Hmm, I haven't told anyone about the OCD. I guess Ava could be a first, I trust her. Even Doc said I should tell a friend and well......Ava's the only one I have. I leave home this morning with an intention. I reach Ava's door waiting for her to come out, more impatient than usual. She comes out and greets me. I greet her back and we talk for 5 minutes until I thought it was the right time.

"Ava, can I tell you something?"

"Anytime, what's going on?"

I tell her about the phobia, the OCD and the psychologist. Excluding the robbery and the blog of course.

She looks at me with watery eyes and THAT FACE.

IT'S THAT FACE. THE ONE I HATE MOST, OH NO EW, GOD!

Eyebrows pointing upwards, almost watery eyes, frowning face, hand on my shoulder.

NO, AVA, PLEASE, NO!

She pities me, doesn't she?

"I- I'm so-so sorry about that, Robbie. Why didn't you ever tell me? I would've helped and supported you. I'm sorry, Robbie. I really am," she empathises.

I HATE THIS.

I feel aggressive. I'm frustrated. The sting at the back of my head shoots up and I start trembling. And then, I get a weird sensation as if I want to harm her. I want to kill Ava. I feel like I want to hurt her.

NO! NO! NO! NO! NO! NO!

I walk ahead of Ava and pace towards school faster without talking to Ava or making eye contact. The moment I'm out of her sight, I take out two pills and swallow them in a rush. I feel so uneasy, almost like I'm nauseous. I rush to class, take a seat there and take deep breaths. The pills make me feel better. I don't know what happened in class very well, I could hardly keep track of what was going on.

All I know is that we have a task to research on recently happened first degree murders, get an insight on them and prove the murderer guilty with evidence that hasn't already been used. That should be interesting. I still feel very bad so I take two more pills and rush home. I enter home and see..........Dad? Is that you? I see dad sitting on the sofa oh my god what? Tears start flowing out of my eyes. I rub my eyes to see if what I was seeing was real.

.......

I was hallucinating. Dad isn't there anymore. I sob softly, I miss dad, I would be doing so much better now if dad was here. I go to my room and freshen up. I research for my task and find out ways that the murder could've happened. After a few hours of work, I go for dinner. I walk to the kitchen and see mom making something.

"Hey mom!" I say lazily.

"Hi Robbie!" she replies back, "Oh Robbie, I forgot to tell you I'll be leaving tomorrow morning for another conference and I'll be back by day after, alright?"

"Mom, really? Mom, whyyyyy? I have so much to do with law school and then I'll have to handle the house and take care of Jonah too, ugh," I complain.

"Sorry sweetie, I got to know about it just recently and I'll be back by day after anyways. It's just for a day," she smiles at me.

Suddenly, I see a knife on the kitchen slab and the weirdest thing ever happens. I feel like I want to kill my own mother? Oh my god, oh my god, what are you doing, Robbie, get a hold of yourself! I rush back to my room and get two pills. I eat dinner in a hurry and go back to my room telling mom I have work to do. What is happening to you, Robbie? Robbie, what have you become? I'm starting to hate myself. I fall asleep so I can present my task properly tomorrow.

# Chapter Twenty-One

The next morning, mom left for her conference, I drop Jonah off at his friend's house and go straight to school without waiting for Ava. The class starts. Everybody has really creative ways of the murder and they present their tasks.

"Roll no. 36 Robbie Wilson" calls out the teacher.

I stand up and go to the front of the class.

I introduce my project, talk about the possibilities and conclude, just as I had imagined the murder, "Person choked, by hand or poisoning of the room, body frozen, snuck into an underground mortuary or buried in a cemetery. Best possible option."

Ouch, my head hurts. For some reason, my throat feels dry, I can't breathe, my chest hurts and I leave the class mid-way sweating and trembling. Something has polluted my mind, something feels really wrong. I rush back home and lock myself in my room. I take two pills and get back to working on some extra tasks I had. I eat dinner with Jonah and realise it's almost time to sleep. The dark, it isn't safe. It feels unprotected. Mom isn't here. What if something happens to Jonah? What if someone does something to him? I think for a while until my head hurts again and I start getting weird thoughts. I feel like I want to kill someone????? I feel like I want to kill anybody. Anyone who comes in front of me. Jonah. I open my drawer and panic.

SHIT!

I check my pocket and rush to my bag to check it.

I have no pills left. NO! NO! NO! NO! NO! NO!

Doc had told me not to have too many of them and now I can't survive without them. What do I do? I hate what's happening. I can't *kill* Jonah, no. I walk to my table, pick up the cutter and run into the bathroom. I bang the door hard and start crying and screaming. AAAAAAAAAAAAAAAAAAAAA!

What have I become? I hate myself. *I've become what I feared most.* I've become a killer. How could I even think of killing Jonah? I can't kill someone. Wait...... I'm already a killer....I already have killed someone. My mind flips around and makes me feel like my brain wants to escape my head. As if another version of me wants to take over.

And then, it all starts to make sense. When I think I'm thinking about death....I'm not really thinking about death, I'm actually thinking about murder. All the tasks, the case files, the nightmares. They all point towards murder. When I think I'm scared of getting killed, I'm actually more scared I might harm someone else. From one incident to the other, I don't think I'll get hurt, instead I'm actually scared I might hurt someone. When I felt aggressive towards Ava, I couldn't control myself. I'm not losing control of myself, I'm losing control of my thoughts.

How can I hurt someone? How can I hurt myself? How have I become exactly what I hated most? Aarggghhhh, feeling overwhelmed and out of control, I take the cutter and stick the blade into the thick skin just below my biceps. AAAAAAAAA!

This hurts. But I want to feel the pain. I'm liking the pain. ROBBIE, WHAT?

What are you doing Robbie? You're enjoying hurting yourself?

NO! NO! NO! NO! NO! NO!

What's happening? What am I doing?

I push in the cutter deeper as blood clots in the area and the pain takes over me.

I slowly pull out the blade and the blood rushes out of my hand, escaping the tense enclosed prison of my skin. I pant fast trying to breathe. I slowly feel more and more violent, it's not going well.

Still drenched in tears, I open the door of the bathroom with a loud swing and come out.

I need my pills. I have no pills. What do I do? I stand just above Jonah on his bed with the cutter blade slid open in my hand. My other hand, still bleeding vigorously, the pain unending making my hand feel detached from my body. Somehow, that isn't bothering me as much as everything else right now though.

Why am I liking hurting people? Why am I enjoying hurting myself? Why do I feel this way?

I'm so out of control.

WHY DO I ENJOY PAIN?

I look towards Jonah and hear a car about 600 yards away turning around the corner.

Wait what? There are no houses in our neighbourhood and no one uses this route in winters. It's only 6.30 AM. Is mom back early? SHIT!

I have no option. I need my pills. I need some help.

What are you doing, Robbie?

Robbie, get a hold of yourself!

I sob even more collapsing on the floor beside Jonah's bed. This is how it was supposed to happen. It was meant to be. It's the end. I can't control myself anymore, it's not my fault. I sigh and get on my feet. Putting my cutter forward, I violently stick it in Jonah's chest. I'm crying and screaming, my throat in my hands, it feels like someone's tearing through my throat to get to my mouth. Until it's done. My chest feels choked but I continue taking the cutter out and repeatedly stabbing it back in. My tears don't stop until I hear the creak of a door. I'm on my knees with Jonah's body in front of me. Blood soaking my hands, both my blood and Jonah's, his torso is covered, his shirt wet in dark red blood, the room stinks of death, the floor soaked with drenching blood spilled and then me, just sitting there on my knees, crying, feeling helpless, feeling hopeless.... It's the end.

This is the end. So I guess, *Life is death.*

*6 months later*

# Epilogue

It's been 6 months since everything happened. I'm writing this from rehab now. 6 months, 180 days, 4320 hours and I still can't process everything that happened. I was weak and gave in to my darker side. Don't we all have that darker side though? There are no 'good people'. It's just about who keeps it in control, you know? I'm getting better now and I'll be fine soon but that didn't come easy. I lost everything and everyone that mattered to me. Jonah, I lost Jonah. Mom, honestly, I'd be surprised if she even talks to me. Ms. Johnson...I disappointed her. Doc.........I don't know, to be honest. The world was shattered and everything was taken away from me in front of my eyes. The only difference was that I, myself, was the one tearing my world apart. I hurt myself more than anyone else did. I hurt my own mother more than anyone else did. I- I hurt Jonah, Ava. Everyone. I shouldn't have taken the pills so impusively, I shouldn't have given in so quick. I know I shouldn't have.....but I lost control. I lost control of my mind, my life, it was like something else was speaking from inside of me....like I could hear this voice in my head telling me what to do. But even after everything, I'm alive, I feel better now, I've almost recovered. Yea, of course, I'd much rather wish Jonah was in place of me, atleast he would've been here. Why'd he have to suffer because of me? It was my fault, I know it and I'm sorry. I really am. I wish I could help it.......because sometimes the aircraft of life comes crash landing on you and you really can't do anything about it.